T0145018

It's All About Being Tough

Written by Rebecca Klar Lusk
Illustrated by Robert E. Klar

Copyright © 2018 Rebecca Klar Lusk.

Scripture quotations are taken from The Living Bible copyright © 1971. Used by permission of
Tyndale House Publishers, Inc., Carol Stream, Illinois 60188. All rights reserved.

All rights reserved. No part of this book may be used or reproduced by any means, graphic, electronic, or mechanical, including photocopying, recording, taping or by any information storage retrieval system without the written permission of the author except in the case of brief quotations embodied in critical articles and reviews.

Interior Image Credit: Robert E. Klar

WestBow Press books may be ordered through booksellers or by contacting:

WestBow Press
A Division of Thomas Nelson & Zondervan
1663 Liberty Drive
Bloomington, IN 47403
www.westbowpress.com
1 (866) 928-1240

Because of the dynamic nature of the Internet, any web addresses or links contained in this book may have changed since publication and may no longer be valid. The views expressed in this work are solely those of the author and do not necessarily reflect the views of the publisher, and the publisher hereby disclaims any responsibility for them.

This is a work of fiction. All of the characters, names, incidents, organizations, and dialogue in
this novel are either the products of the author's imagination or are used fictitiously.

Any people depicted in stock imagery provided by Getty Images are models, and
such images are being used for illustrative purposes only.
Certain stock imagery © Getty Images.

ISBN: 978-1-9736-4024-0 (sc)
ISBN: 978-1-9736-4025-7 (e)

Library of Congress Control Number: 2018911152

Print information available on the last page.

WestBow Press rev. date: 09/28/2018

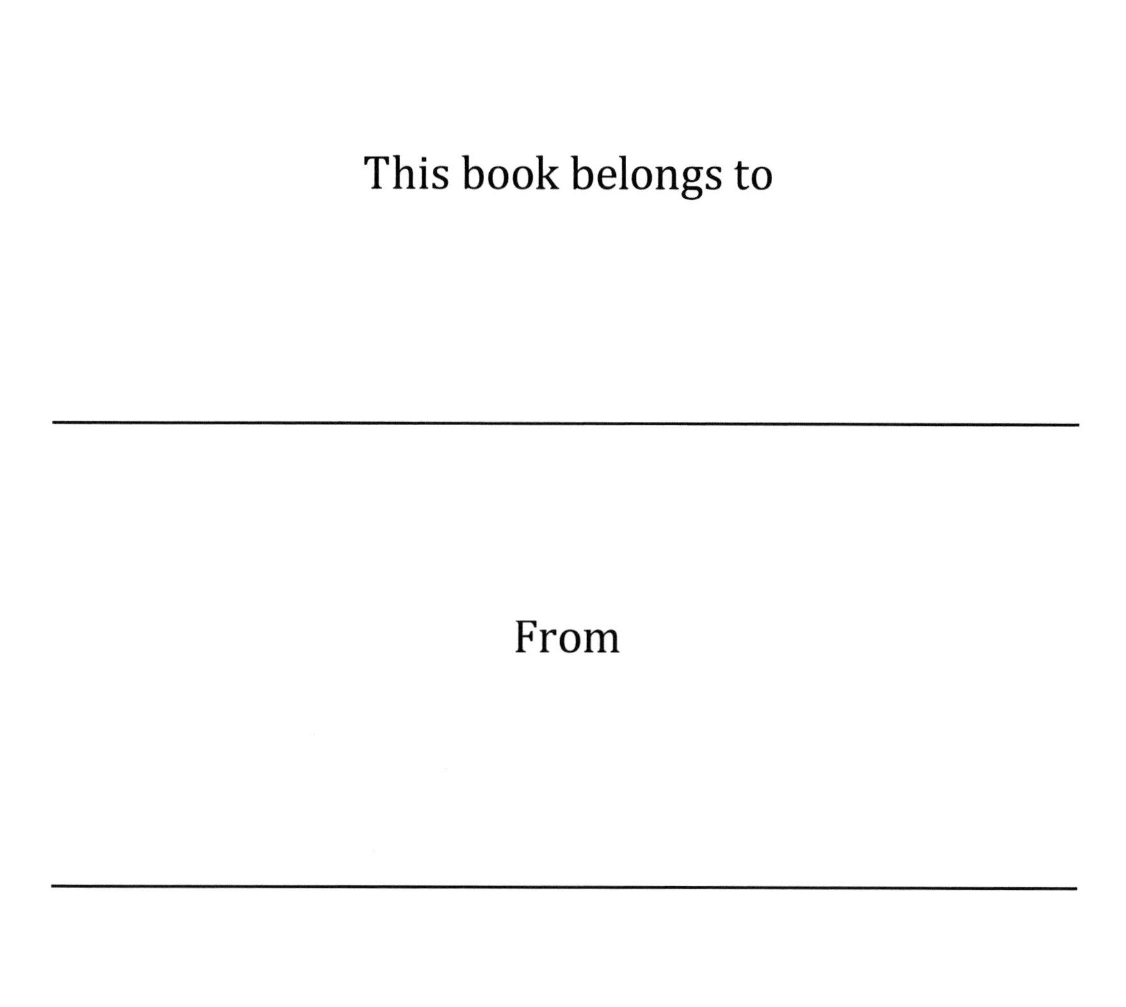
This book belongs to
From

For Eli Truman Lusk and Everly Christine
Lusk, my treasured grandchildren.

This, the fifth "It's All About" book, is another
reminder that whether you're Tall, Small, Strong,
Tough, or Smart, It's All About Jesus in your heart!

Each book honors the life and memory of my son, Christopher
Paul Lusk, as he truly demonstrated the love of Jesus in *his*
heart. He loved serving the Lord, and fully believed that
God created and loved each of us as unique individuals.

You are loved unconditionally by your creator.
May you know Him personally in your heart.

Special Thanks

A thank you to Phylis Marie Klar, mother to me, the author, and my brother, the illustrator. Our mom, at the age of 96, is still persevering through life, and she has demonstrated over the years, an example of being TOUGH in a commendable fashion.

Toughness saw her through a battle with polio at age 5, and it has carried her through life all of these years. Thanks, mom for passing on character traits that have helped us in our lives.

Hard work, determination, tenacity, working against the odds, and having faith in God has helped carry us through.

“It’s all about being
tough,” laughed
the hyena,

To all of those he met.

“It’s all about being
tough that’s important,

And don’t you ever forget.”

"Being tough gives
me more chances
To act cool with others around.
I sometimes even tease them.
They get quiet and don't
make a sound."

"Because I'm **tough** I push and shove
On the playground and in my classroom.
Others are alarmed and I make them shake.
I'll never get knocked down, kaboom!"

"I never fear those
who are bigger,
To me they are not a threat.
Even those who have
more strength
Have not overpowered
me yet."

"It's all about being **tough**," I say.
"I can put others down in a jiffy.
My harsh words always get to them.
They all dash away quite swiftly."

"Challenging others
to me is amusing.
I can put down anyone.
Since I'm so tough
they don't take a chance.
Off they go on a fast-paced run."

"Yes it's all about
being **tough**.

When I speak others
listen to me.

I always get in
the last word.

No one argues, they
all just agree."

"I can be tough
during the day.
I keep active
throughout the night.
There isn't
anyone I fear.
I take pleasure in
giving others fright."

"I'm a champ at being **tough**.
I laugh while I put others down.
There has never been another
Who could cause this **tough** one to frown."

"It's all about being **tough**,"
laughed the hyena.
"Others shudder when they look at me."
Then out of nowhere a lion cub appeared,
And he scratched the hyena's knee.

"It's all about being **tough**?"
roared the cub.
"Being brave is what matters more."
The hyena frowned and hobbled away,
Head hanging low with a
knee that was sore.

God tells us in His Word that all of us are special. Being tough is not the best thing, for God loves each and every one of us just the way we are. After all, God made us. We are His creation, and He is the maker of all good things. Be yourself, and be thankful for all that you are. God loves each of us unconditionally. That means His love for us will never change.

He sent His son to die for us on a cross. It's really ALL ABOUT KNOWING JESUS. He gives us what we need. Jesus and God His father are a team. If you haven't asked Jesus into your heart, do it right now. Accepting Jesus as your personal Lord and Savior is the most important life decision you will ever make. Through Him you have eternal life. That's a life that goes on forever in heaven.

Hallelujah for

JESUS!

Vocabulary

1. Important – Meaningful and valuable.
2. Cool – Being attractive, stylish, impressive.
3. Kaboom – To crash, sudden change (fall down).
4. Threat – Intending to cause pain or injury.
5. Jiffy – To do something quickly.
6. Challenging – Difficult in a way that's interesting.
7. Agree – To have the same thought or opinion.
8. Pleasure – To have a happy feeling.
9. Champ – A winner (short for champion).
10. Shudder – To shake because of fear.
11. hobbled – To walk with a limp, often due to pain.

Praise and Prayer

Give God Praise if you are tough.
That's how He created you.
He designed you with much love
And He knows what you can do.

Always remember, He looks inside
To see what's in your heart.
He desires for you to accept Jesus,
And never grow apart.

It's really all about knowing JESUS
That matters most of all.
God wants you to accept His Son,
Whether you're tough, strong, smart, small, or tall.

Invite Jesus into your heart today.
Say this simple prayer.
Just be how God created you.
And serve Him everywhere.

Dear Jesus,

I need you in my life. I know you died for me on the cross because of your love for me. Come into my life and live in my heart. Forgive me for the things I have done wrong. I want to follow you and know more about you. You have done something wonderful for me. Let me live for you. Thank you, Amen.

Laugh and Learn

What kind of joke do you tell to a spotted hyena? It doesn't matter, they laugh at it anyway!

How many words can you make using the letters in **spotted hyena**? Example: **eyes.**

Learning Activities

1. Get some note cards and make flash cards using words from this book.
2. Can you list an animal starting with all 26 letters of the alphabet?
3. Write down your name and give a positive adjective for each letter. (adjectives describe something) Example: SAM – Smiley, Alert, Mannerly. Try this for other names of family or friends. Use kindness when describing someone.
4. Find and list at least twelve nouns used in this story. (noun: person, place, or thing)
5. Search for rhyming words in this book. (words ending in the same sounds) Example: tall and small.
6. Search for Bible verses using the word hyena.
7. Find a star on the hyena's scarf.

True or False Facts

1. Hyenas are smarter than chimps.
2. Hyenas kill baby lions.
3. The spotted hyena is not the largest hyena.
4. Hyenas live only in Africa.
5. There are four types of hyenas.
6. Baby hyenas are called cubs.
7. Spotted hyenas often hunt in groups.
8. The hyena is not a nocturnal animal.
9. The spotted hyena is called the laughing hyena.
10. Cubs are born with no teeth and eyes closed.

Answers: 1T, 2T, 3F, 4F, 5T, 6T, 7T, 8F, 9T, 10F

YOUR DRAWING LESSON

All drawings begin with a basic shape or shapes and a few simple lines. Create one of the animals you find in your book using the shapes and lines you see below. After drawing and coloring this picture, get some more paper and draw other animals of your own.

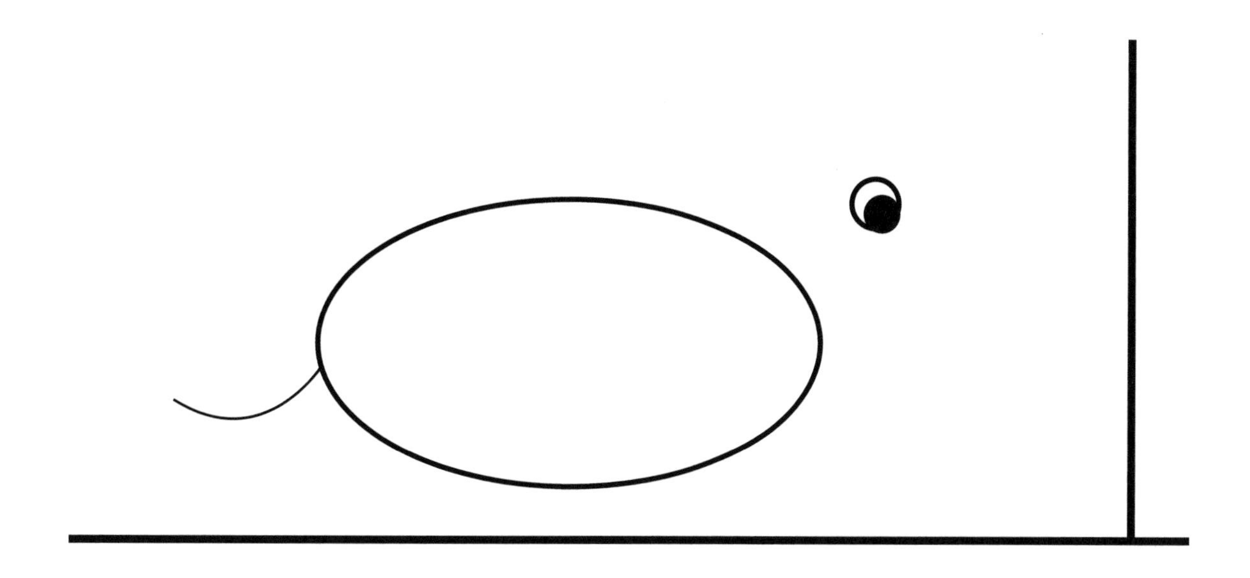

Printed in the United States
By Bookmasters